This book
belongs to

. . . .

Fun Ideas for the Storyteller

Where's Bitesize? is a delightful family story. Children will easily be able to relate to Bitesize's dilemma. The fun, the hiding game, and the touch of fear have such appeal that you will need to be ready to read the story again and again.

Read on to find out how to get the most fun out of this story.

Reading in parts

There is a lot of repetition in the text. This makes it easier for children to participate in the reading and to predict what will happen next. Encourage your child to be Bitesize and to say his whispered words, *"Under the bed. So you will never never find me"* while you take on the role of Bitesize's mum and dad.

Look at the bubbles

Help your child understand that the words in the bubbles are those the characters are saying – this will follow easily if your child has started to say Bitesize's words. Point to the words in bubbles, read them, and ask who is speaking. Encourage your child to think about how the dialogue is said. For example, *"Oh Bitesize, where are you?"* would be said in a rather worried voice.

Hiding under the bed

Although Bitesize has a sore paw and is a bit frightened, the story is really a humorous one. The pictures bring out the fun in the text. Look at them together, and laugh at Bitesize's antics. Your child might be curious about why Bitesize is hiding under the bed. This is a great chance to talk with your child about what to do if she gets hurt.

Favourite hiding places

Bitesize's parents look everywhere they can think of for him but only his friend Minta knows where he is. As you look at the book a second time ask your child to list the places mentioned and then talk about hiding places. Does your child have a favourite place to escape to? She may want to keep it secret of course!
A game of hide-and-seek is a perfect way to end sharing this story.

Enjoy this glimpse into Bitesize's life and the games that follow too!

Wendy Cooling

Wendy Cooling
Reading Consultant

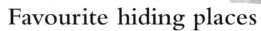

For Rooby Doo and Luce with fondest love – IW
For the racoons of Fulmer – PD

Dorling **DK** Kindersley

LONDON, NEW YORK, SYDNEY, DELHI, PARIS,
MUNICH and JOHANNESBURG

First published in Great Britain in 2001
by Dorling Kindersley Limited,
9 Henrietta Street, London WC2E 8PS

2 4 6 8 10 9 7 5 3 1

Text copyright © 2001 Ian Whybrow
Illustrations copyright © 2001 Penny Dann

A CIP catalogue record for this book is available from the British Library.
ISBN 0-7513-2888-X
Colour reproduction by Dot Gradations, UK
Printed in China by Wing King Tong

Edited by Sarah Walker
Designed by Venice Shone

Acknowledgements:
Series Reading Consultant: Wendy Cooling **Series Activities Advisor:** Lianna Hodson
Photographer: Trisha Gant **Models:** Mrs Singh, Sheila Singh, Arjan Singh, Ghobin Singh, Zachary D'Arcy

For our complete
catalogue visit
www.dk.com

Where's Bitesize?

by Ian Whybrow • illustrated by Penny Dann

A Dorling Kindersley Book

Supper was on the table
when Bitesize came by.
Fast.

Racoon Ti[r]

742 163

Do you recognize him?

MASKED BANDIT
SOUGHT

Bandit Raids
Farmer Jones
Barn

Hi, Bitesize,

said Dad.
But he missed him.

"Was that Bitesize?" said Mum,
busy with the bread.
"Maybe he went to wash his hands,"
said Dad, busy with the newspaper.
"Who, Bitesize? Wash his hands?"
said Mum. "I don't think so."

"You're right," said Dad. "I'll go and get him."
And off he went to look for him.

Bitesize, Supper!

He looked in all the usual places in the house.

He looked in the garden.

He looked in the shed.

And Bitesize whispered,

Under the bed. So you will never never find me.

"I can't find him," said Dad.
"Will you help me, Honey?"
And off they went to
look for him again.

"Let's look in the cupboard."

"No, not here."

"He may be here instead."

"No, not here."

Oh, Bitesize, where are you?

And Bitesize whispered,

Under the bed. So you will never <u>never</u> find me.

"I'm worried," said Mum.

"Maybe he went back to Minta's house," said Dad.

So off they went
to find him.

When they got to Minta's house, Minta was in the bath blowing bubbles.

And Minta's Mum said, "Your Bitesize came this afternoon to play with Araminta. They had fun in the treehouse and then he got a splinter.

I went to fetch a needle and suddenly he fled. I *wonder* where he's hiding."

And Minta said,

I
know.

And everybody said,

Where?

And Minta said,

Under
the bed!

So Mum and Dad hurried back home.

Mum and Dad crept up the stairs,
careful not to squeak,

"This way, quietly. . . shhh. Don't speak!"

They dangled down a chocolate bar
on a bit of thread.

And out came a paw from . . .
    under the bed.

Tweak with the tweezers.

Got it!

Mum said.

Ow!

said a voice from . . .
under the bed.

And Mum and Dad said,
"How is your paw now?"
And Bitesize said,
"It's better, but still a little sore."

So Mum and Dad said,
"Do you think you could manage
just a *little* bit of supper?"
And a little voice said,

So guess where they all had
supper that evening. . .

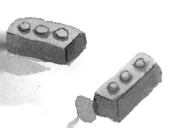

Under the bed! Deeeeeelish!

Activities to Enjoy

If you've enjoyed this story, you might like to try some of these simple, fun activities with your child.

Make a playhouse

Bitesize and Minta play in their treehouse. Bitesize hides under his bed. Think about where your child likes to play and hide. She can make a den so that she has her own special hiding place!

Making Masks

On a piece of card or paper, draw the shape of Bitesize's face. The Bitesize family are racoons, and have long snouts with shiny black noses and dark rings around their eyes.

Start off by drawing a circle with two triangles on top. Use pens, crayons, or sticky paper to make the features on your mask.

Glue or tape a short stick to the centre of the back of the mask. Now your child has her own Bitesize mask!

Communication

Think about the ways in which the characters communicate in the story. For example they call out to one another when they are searching for Bitesize, and reassure him that everything is okay when they find him hiding underneath the bed.

What other ways can your child think of to communicate? Why not try something new, such as making a telephone out of two yoghurt pots and some string? Inventing a secret code is also fun.

1 Chop the fruit into small pieces. Your child may need help with this. Layer the ingredients in the glass, starting with the pineapple, then banana, raspberries, yoghurt, and ice cream.

Favourite treats

As well as chocolate, another of Bitesize's favourite treats is this fruit sundae.

Fruit Sundae

To make a delicious sundae you will need these ingredients:

2 cups of pineapple pieces
1 cup of raspberries or strawberries
1 cup of fruit-flavoured yoghurt
1 cup of vanilla ice cream
1 banana, peeled and sliced
Chocolate sauce and hundreds and thousands to decorate.

You will also need a sundae glass and a long spoon to eat with!

2 Keep adding until your glass is full. Decorate your sundae with chocolate sauce and hundreds and thousands!

Yummy!

Other Share-a-Story books to enjoy:

Clara and Buster Go Moondancing
by Dyan Sheldon, illustrated by Caroline Anstey

Mama Tiger, Baba Tiger
by Juli Mahr, illustrated by Graham Percy

I Like Me
by Laurence Anholt, illustrated by Adriano Gon

Not Now, Mrs Wolf!
by Shen Roddie, illustrated by Selina Young

Are You Spring?
by Caroline Pitcher, illustrated by Cliff Wright

The Caterpillar That Roared
by Michael Lawrence, illustrated by Alison Bartlett

Nigel's Numberless World
by Lucy Coats, illustrated by Neal Layton